The Walls of Madness
by
Craig Saunders

Copyright © 2011 Craig Saunders

All characters in this novel are fictitious and any resemblance to persons, living or dead, is entirely coincidental.

The moral right of the author has been asserted.

All rights reserved.

No part of this publication may be reproduced, stored in a retrieval system, or transmitted, in any form or by any means without the prior permission in writing of the publisher, nor be otherwise circulated in any form of binding or cover or format other than that in which it is published and without similar condition including this condition being imposed on the subsequent purchase.

2nd Edition

1st Edition published 2012 by Crowded Quarantine Publications
Edited by Adam Millard

Cover Art Copyright © 2015 Craig Saunders

ISBN 13: 978-1973259060

CONTENTS

Part One
Part Two
Part Three

About the Author
Also by Craig Saunders

Part One

One of the many worst things about being nuts was being so goddamned important.

Mark Vonnegut
The Eden Express: A Memoir of Insanity

I.

When Billy Hunter saw spiders in the walls, it was Eileen Westwood that chased them away with broom or duster. Billy saw spiders, and beetles, and mice, sometimes. Sometimes it was different, and it wasn't any of those things. Those times Eileen didn't go rushing in, because Billy wasn't right in the head then.

Good lord, that didn't sound Christian, but Billy wasn't right in the head and that was the best that could be said. Sweetest man she'd ever met when it was just the creepies and the crawlies and the scrabbling in the walls, but when the black moon was on him, when the Devil was in him ranting at the black moon…

Well, those times, she took a knife in her pocket along with her broom or duster and prayed to the Good Lord for the poor man.

She took the knife not because he was a danger to her. Never that.

No. She took it because he could be persuasive enough that he got her scared of the things in the walls, too. Those things he saw, she didn't ever want to see.

But he wasn't right in the head, and there were no such things as the Hatheth or the Krama, the Yik and the man, the Marlin.

'No.'

There were no such things.

'No,' she said. She spoke out loud, because she thought it'd do her good to hear the words, but there was doubt in her voice. She knew why. Even though it was nuts, it was because he could be damn convincing. Some days she chased those things away while he screamed and raved and tried to climb the wall behind her, his heels scrabbling at the walls. He'd clawed that wall so many times his fingernails were all broken and torn. The blood on the walls he washed down – she was hot on creepies, but not so good with blood.

'Poor, poor man,' she said, shaking her head. He didn't deserve what happened to him. Maybe his old man had it in his blood, the sickness, just like his son. Billy never did talk about his dad, though, nor his mum, for that matter. But it was a shame, alright. Smart boy, hitting the prime of his life…could happen to anyone, she supposed. Not her. She had her rock, and that was the all of it.

But Billy suffered. Grown man or not, he cried those nights, and shrieked, too, sometimes, in a high pitch that dug needles into her spine.

The man, the Marlin, though. He came on the worst of days and Good Lord didn't he scare her? Did he? Of course he did, because when he came she didn't mind admitted she'd needed the toilet really badly.

Just kind of like night terrors, for Billy. It had become a lullaby for her, ever since he moved in. But she loved the boy and it wasn't the Marlin tonight, just the low beasts, the beetles, maybe the mice…she couldn't tell anything from the scream except that it wasn't *them*. It wasn't *him*.

And that wasn't so bad.

Just plain screaming, like kid who'd just had a nightmare. She could deal with that, easy as. She almost smiled.

Eileen checked the old school clock on the wall. 11pm.

Good time. Get in early and sometimes she could read a little before bed, after Billy'd calmed down a little.

She pulled on her wellies and her overcoat in the front porch, because winter was just about kicking in. Middle of December and they still got the occasional sunshine day, but cold enough now.

Old bones, but she always was good with the cold.

Just a short hop over the fence and she'd be next door and with any luck she wouldn't be listening to him through the wall all night.

She loved Billy like a neighbour should, but she still liked her sleep.

Coat on, wellies pulled up smartly over her tights, she kissed the little cross that hung down between low breasts and picked up the broom for some chasing.

*

II.

A mouse skittered around the skirting board and popped into a hole. There was a greasy line around the skirting board, marking out their run. Didn't matter how often Bill put down traps and poison. Didn't matter how often he blocked the hole. They gnawed their way through.

They'd gnawed through polyfilla, then polyfilla stacked with mouse poison, wire wool, a small plank he'd nailed in (when Mrs. Westwood was out one day).

He knew mice and rats gnawed things. He knew they were dirty little bastards. But he'd never know them to be invulnerable to every torture known to man.

They lived in the walls. The snuck under the bed while he tried to sleep and cried, some nights, like a little boy afraid of something in the cupboard, crying for Daddy, crying monster.

But it was just mice, and Mrs. Westwood was coming. Billy's chills fled. He could hear her boots, clumping up the old stairs, the stairs creaking. Third step, fourth, seventh, ninth…a couple more to go. Those narrow old stairs with their worn old wood.

For each step his heart slowed a beat. Racing, down to…not quite idling, but maybe an engine settling in for a long stretch on the motorway.

'Billy? What is it?' Mrs. Westwood said, coming into the room. Every light in the room blazed – A harsh bulb with no shade hung from the ceiling, a bedside lamp, and a standing lamp there in the corner.

He felt calmer already, but he could still hear them.

'Mrs Westwood…I'm sorry…I'm…'

'Good boy,' she said, like she was talking to one of her pupils, back before she'd retired. 'Good boy. Just tell me where those little…'

'Mice,' he said. 'Mouse. Just one. It went into the hole in the wall. It's in the walls. I can't sleep…I can't sleep…'

'Ssh,' she said, and held her broom out in front of her. She could sense him building up again. See it in his eyes, the way he worked his jaw and somehow seemed to bite his own teeth while he spoke, like he couldn't remember the size of his own mouth, nor how to make the words in his head fit through it.

'Show me,' she said, and remembered not to lead him, just to follow. It could make it worse if she got to the wall before he pointed it out. It was always the same thing, on creepies and crawlies nights – the hole.

There wasn't any hole there, but Eileen Westwood went exactly where Billy pointed, nonetheless. He'd nailed a bit of board over the non-existent hole some time ago, so it would have been easy enough to get there first. But she didn't pre-empt him. She just followed his lead.

'Shoo!' she said eventually. 'Shoo!' Like she meant it, like she was really angry at all mice and seriously pissed off with this one in particular.

She flapped the broom at the hole that wasn't there. Sometimes she felt like an idiot, but these kinds of nights when Billy was pretty much as there as he ever got after dark, she didn't mind so much. It wasn't a frightening thing. She just waved the broom around, or the duster, and things went away from Billy's head.

Once or twice there had been actual spiders, but she'd flattened those pretty quickly. Apart from once, this massive spider, all spindly legs, that moved way too fast for her old bones. She wasn't a slouch. She was pretty nimble for seventy, though she tried not to be prideful of it. Still, that damn spider had been quick.

'Shoo!' she shouted at the hole that wasn't there. Billy came a little closer.

'It's gone?'

'It's gone,' she nodded. A lot of times just her reassurance or maybe the tone of her voice was enough to settle him down.

'Didn't see the other ones?'

Oh, she thought. Stave it off and quickly. Don't question, don't get into anything uncomfortable.

'Nothing,' she said. 'A mouse, and that's all, and it's gone now. Now you can go to sleep.' She kept her voice calm, but firm, too, like she wasn't going to take any kind of argument.

She saw Billy was crying a bit, even though he was a man of thirty.

But then he wasn't like normal men. He used to be a teacher himself. He'd got a degree in history and even went on to get a master's degree. That was before his breakdown.

Schizophrenia, they called it, but she didn't really know much about that, apart from what she'd looked up in the library. It was pretty rare, thank God.

It didn't matter what textbooks said. All she knew was that the poor man suffered, and that the mouse was gone, and that she had a cup of tea going cold and a book waiting.

But Good Lord, that wasn't charitable.

Still…

'All right, Billy? You can sleep now. I've got to go to sleep myself. I'm driving you in the morning? Remember?'

Billy wasn't allowed to drive, because of his illness or his medication, she didn't know. But he wasn't allowed to drive and he was her neighbour, so she drove him, and if she was honest with herself she sort of enjoyed the company and yes, the purpose, too.

It wasn't so easy, growing old alone, out in the country. Schizophrenic or not, Billy was a good man when he was in himself. Toughest was the nights, but the night was done now and in the morning he'd probably be just fine, or near enough so as a good neighbour wouldn't make a big deal out of it.

'Thank you. Thank you,' he said. 'Eileen…I'm sorry. So sorry.'

'Ssh, now. None of that. You'll be fine. It was just a mouse and nothing to be frightened off, OK?'

Billy nodded. She nodded back, satisfied he'd be alright. The terror was fading from his eyes, and he was beginning to look sleepy. Relief, or medication kicking in, she didn't know. Didn't matter either way, though, because he was going to go off and she was going to get some sleep.

That was good enough.

'I'm going to go now, all right?'

'Sorry.'

'Enough,' she said, in that same firm tone she'd learned long and hard in the school rooms of her working years.

She nodded once again before she clomped back down the stairs.

She stepped over the fence between their properties and into her back garden. She'd thought about maybe laying some slabs there, so she didn't have to wear her wellies. She never quite got round to it.

Her tea was cold when she got back, but she boiled up the kettle and took a fresh cup to bed. Her bed was cold, but she had a thick nightie and she kind of liked the feel of cold crisp sheets on her bare feet. She always had, right since she'd been a little girl.

Eileen Westwood read for an hour or so, set her mental alarm clock for five, and went out like a light.

*

III.

Bill woke at eight when the alarm on his mobile phone went off.

He rolled his tongue around in his head, groaned a little as he tried to work some moisture into his mouth. His evening pills made his head thick like it was full of cold, and his mouth feel like it was full of candyfloss, but maybe more like candyfloss made from spider's webs.

He shook his head. Morning light, and he wasn't going down that road. Not today. There weren't any spiders, not in the daylight. And not the other things.

Bill lay for a few seconds, trying to work his brain up, fell asleep again. His mobile was on snooze.

They can come in the day, too.

He jumped at the thought, half-dreamt.

Normally he'd sleep in 'til ten, maybe eleven. But today wasn't one of those days. Today was a hospital day, and he sort of looked forward to those, because for a while after talking things through, he felt better. Never all the way, but the demons in his head popped out, hung around his psychologist for a while. At least, that's how he imagined it working. He saw them, sometimes, the spiders and the spider things and the Yik and the Krama, crawling, seeping, sliding, out of his brain and down his shoulders, trails of slime and ichor...

But he wasn't going there. Stop.

He took the circle in his head and snapped it. New day, new start. Fuck the circle. Fuck his brain.

'Faa,' he said. Pushed himself out of bed, into the toilet, pissed and brushed his teeth. Only then did he manage to say it.

'Fuck you, brain,' he said through a mouthful of toothpaste and spat out the drug shit that caked his mouth into the sink.

He took fresh clothes from the chest of drawers and the wardrobe. He pulled on his underwear and socks and trousers first, then the top half. The room was cold, frost on the single pane windows. With the heating on the frost would turn to water and run and add to the black rot seeping through the old wooden frames.

He padded in his socks to the landing and down the stairs. His house had just one bedroom, but he'd never need more. He knew he wouldn't be living out a life growing old with a wife he loved and doted on right into old age. He'd die alone.

It made him sad, and he didn't want to feel sad so early in the morning.

He took his morning cocktail before breakfast – Olanzapine and Pericyazine, both on the maximum dose. Didn't seem to help him much, but he had to admit, during the day, he could kind of function. Sometimes he saw things…things he didn't like to think about in the light of day, things that only crept up on him when the light failed and the shadows came out…but he could shut his eyes to those things when it was light and the shadows still moved fast enough that *they* couldn't come through.

The low beasts.

But they weren't here, and he didn't need to think about them for a while. It was going to be a good day.

Bill ate a breakfast of two muffins with fried bacon and fried eggs and two slices of cheese each and black pepper. When he'd finished his breakfast he lit his first cigarette of the day while the kettle boiled.

Being fat, getting cancer…didn't really matter, did it? He had bigger things to worry about. Living as a schizophrenic was hard e-fucking-nuff.

'Hard e-fucking-nuff,' he said.

He drank tea and sat at the table in his small kitchen, looking out over the barren fields, the stick trees along the boundaries between fields. The other side, out the front of the house, the road ran by, but on either side were fields. A few trees seemed to cling to the clouds, with their wide branches like fingers dug into flesh.

The clouds raced by but the sun poked through a couple of times while he smoked his second cigarette and drank his first cup of tea and tried not to think about mice and beetles and bugs and the other things that were dark and some of those things that could talk and told him they wanted him.

They needed him, they said. They had great work for him, they said.

He didn't listen, but then the other side told him things that frightened him. Sometimes they showed themselves and on those nights he screamed.

But that didn't matter now, because he was going to the hospital, and Eileen'd be with him, and maybe one day soon things would be better, because he was seeing a psychologist now and she'd told him it was going to be alright. Everything was going to be alright.

Maybe she worked for the other side. Maybe she didn't. But he had to take a chance on someone, because even on his worst nights, he knew Eileen wouldn't be around forever, and he was in serious trouble.

*

IV.

'Morning, Mrs. Westwood,' he said, standing in front of his neighbour's door. Sometimes she knocked at his door, sometimes he knocked at hers. Hers was a lot nicer than his. She kept her little cottage immaculate. In the summer flowers hung in baskets either side of her front door. In the winter, like now, she had some kind of trailing plant hanging down, with reddish leaves. It looked good. Looked inviting.

She raised her eyebrow at him.

'Eileen,' he said, with a tired smile. It'd take him 'til midday, at least, until he'd be anything like firing on all cylinders.

Well, never that. The problem was that he had too many cylinders. He really didn't want to be firing them all at once. That's what the medication was for.

'I'm sorry about last night,' he said.

'Billy, don't be daft. Don't start the day out daft, all right?'

He laughed. 'OK, Eileen. I'll try not to. You ready?'

'I'm ready,' she said. 'Just got to get my coat on. You going to stand out there, or come in?'

'Come in, I guess,' he said, and stepped over the threshold. She headed off to the back of the cottage where she kept her coat. She hardly ever used the front door, but Bill didn't feel quite right using the back. He'd known her for three years, give or take, and it still didn't feel right, though he was careful to always leave his own back door open, should she ever want to come in. Should he need her and her broom.

The postman pulled up while she went to the back porch to fetch her coat.

'Morning, Mr. Hunter.'

'How are you, David?'

'Not too bad. Yourself?'

'I'm fine. Fine,' he said as he held out his hand. David passed him his post and Eileen's, too.

'See you later.'

He drove off, his little red van's wheels grating on the gravel drive, off on his rounds.

Eileen came back and Bill passed the post to her.

'Are you ready now?'

'Are you being cheeky with me, young man?'

'Might be,' said Bill with a grin.

Eileen shook her head. 'Kids.'

'I'm thirty, you know.'

'Oh, don't I know it. The big kids were always the worst.'

'That's the truth,' he said.

Bill closed her front door behind them while she clicked the key for her car to unlock. They got in and she reversed out onto the road. The gravel crunched under her tyres. She drove slow, but fast enough to catch and pass David, the postman, on his rounds. They both waved. David waved back.

They came to the first T-junction, marked with a big black and white checked board, there to stop idiots flying straight out and hitting a big tree behind it. There must have been plenty of people who'd done it to warrant that big black and white board.

There weren't any road signs, but then often there weren't in Norfolk. Back during WWII the road signs had been removed, in case the Germans invaded.

Somehow or other, no one seemed to ever get around to replacing them.

They knew the way well enough, though. East it was, east up the coast, and to the community hospital.

*

V.

Bill said goodbye to Eileen in the car park and headed through the main door in the old community hospital toward his appointment, and maybe a short cessation of the night terrors, a small holiday from the circle that went round all day in his head even when he felt pretty straight.

Thing was, even when he felt straight, it didn't mean he was.

That's what the therapy was about. Touch base, check in with reality. Talk therapy, they called it, but it wasn't that, not for him.

He thought of himself more as a kind of Typhoid Mary, wandering through those old thick wooden doors, leaking his poison as he passed. He gave it to the woman at the counter as he checked in on the psychiatric wing of the hospital as an outpatient, thank God. Once he'd been an inpatient, but not here, in this little hospital. They didn't hold nuts here. Just down the road in Norwich, but not here.

He showed his appointment letter. The woman took the letter and typed his hospital number into her terminal. A small spider skittered down Bill's arm and he brushed it off. She looked up at him, but he masked it with a smile. One down, he thought.

He could handle the thought of those spiders and crawling things in the day. Didn't mind if he dropped a few, but he felt a bit guilty about it, too. Like he shouldn't be doing what they told him to, late at night, but the thing of it was, he felt better when he did what they told him, and worse when he wouldn't.

It didn't make any kind of sense, but the woman he saw, Dr. Richards, she didn't mind. She told him if he wanted to drop off some of his nightmares, she didn't mind at all.

It did seem kind of rude, now he thought about it, dropping a spider on the receptionist. He thought about reaching down and plucking his nightmare back off her woollen sleeve, but then thought better of it. She might think he was crazy, or she might think he was about to jump on her. She had bold red hair and her breasts pushed against a white uniform. He imagined her in her underwear, for a moment. Then he felt guilty about that, too. What if she knew what he was thinking?

Then he caught himself. Reached into his head and broke the circle. When she waved him through he smiled at her, and this time his smiled felt a little more genuine, had a little more warmth, and she smiled back.

He knew he hadn't shaved. He knew he was fat, and probably smelled of Marlboro Lights, but he couldn't do anything about that. The least he could do was be polite.

Sometimes he thought people might know if he thought bad things, so he tried to be polite, but he knew that, too, was part of the circle, and for now, that was broken.

The receptionist buzzed him through to the next room. He went in and took a seat and waited.

The thing of it was, it was never off. Never. Even during the days, when it was in the background, it was always on. Like a TV in the front room, sometimes, while he was off making dinner. Always there. In the background, a drone. But at night…

Well, then the volume was turned way up. But for now it was daytime, and Dr. Richards was standing in front of him holding her hand out.

'William? You look well.'

'And you, Doctor.'

'Thank you,' she said, with a warm smile. He never did know whether that smile was real or bought and paid for by the National Health Service.

'You want to come through?'

'Sure,' he nodded.

Session start. One hour, counting down. She knew when an hour was up, exactly. He'd never once caught her checking her watch, but if his mind was like a tricycle on a roundabout, hers must be like a metronome.

*

VI.

Dr. Richards sat with her right leg crossed over her left, knees adjacent, calves parallel.

Her body faced Bill. She held no notes, had her hands folded politely in her lap. Bill sat with his ankles crossed, right foot pointing toward the door and not Dr. Richards, not because he was combative, but because he had long legs and it was a small room and the chair was uncomfortable. He crossed his arms, but only because he didn't have anywhere else to put them, because there were no arms on the chair.

'William, thank you for coming.'

First name, good start. Already her dress – white flowers on red, small bow on her left breast, like a brooch made of material – was covered with *them*.

'Nice to see you. I suppose. Be nice when I don't have to. You know. Not that you're not nice. You are. I just...'

Break the circle, start again.

'Anyway, thanks. What did you want to talk about today?'

Not your place, Bill. Let her run it. Slow down. Go slow over the bumps. Mind your chassis.

'I thought we'd talk about how you're feeling today...anxious, nervous...angry?'

'I hardly ever get angry,' he said, watching the window, the windowsill. Trying to go slow.

'But do you ever get angry?'

'Not often,' he said, shrugging. He watched them crawling over her from the corner of his eye. Watched them swarming across the room.

'Not never, though?'

'Well, no. Not never.'
'How deep does it go, William?'
'What?'
'When was the last time?'
'The last time?'
'When was the last time you were angry?'

Bill tried to think about it. He really did. But he could feel them, now. He bit down. Shrugged.

'You don't want to talk about that?'

No, that wasn't it at all. It wasn't that he didn't want to talk about anger. It was that he couldn't concentrate on squeezing them out of his brain and talk at the same time. Truth be told, it was hard, trying not to look at Dr. Richards' chest. Thinking, 'chest'. That was hard. It was hard to think polite, all the time. Just in case. Harder still to think with the Hatheth pushing their way through his scalp. He couldn't feel pain, not exactly, but…something. Something gross, but not quite. Repulsive, but good, at the same time. Like release, like the rare occasions he masturbated, maybe thought about Dr. Richards, the only woman he saw regularly, really, apart from Eileen. Tried not to think about Eileen while he was thinking about masturbating and Dr. Richards and all the time the Hatheth were coming forth and pouring across the floor and crawling, segmented legs kind of clacking against each other, ungainly, but swift, crawling up her leg.

'OK, we don't have to talk about that,' she said.
'Good.'
'Seven?'
'What?'
'How deep does it go, William? Seven?'

'What?' Bill shook his head. He was getting confused. Shook his head again and closed his eyes.

'Is there anything you'd like to talk about?' sighed Dr. Richards.

Yes, he thought. Yes, there is. But I can't fucking concentrate.

How long have I been in here? How long have I been thinking…ah, fuck. Fuck.

Break the fucking circle, Bill, break it, break it.

He started crying.

'What the hell is wrong with me?'

'There's nothing wrong with you, Bill. Your mind is a little unusual, that's all. It's OK to be upset.' She passed him a tissue from her bag, and he took it. He didn't do anything with it, but it was nice to have something to hold while the tears ran down his face.

'I know you said to break the circle, and I try, but sometimes I break it, then I'm right back in there, in the middle of the circle, and it's whirling round my head. You know? No. You probably don't. But when I'm in the circle, it's harder to break out. When it's just in my head, I can kind of squish it, see? But outside…it's too fucking…sorry…too big. Too hard.'

'OK,' she said.

He shook his head to loosen up. He could feel his neck muscles bunching. When he spoke his teeth clacked together, sometimes, because of the drugs. When he didn't take the drugs his teeth clacked together, too, but because he was speaking so fast.

'Every night, they're there. During the day, I cope. Kind of. Maybe. But nights are worse. Can you, you know…is there something else?'

'What are you on, now? Dosage?'

He told her. Morning meds, evening meds.

She jotted these down on a pad from her bag. Looked at them for a while and pursed her lips.

'We're scraping around here, William. I won't lie to you. You haven't responded well. There are options, though,' she said, and he sat forward.

'I'll try it.'

'Well…'

He pounced, just in case she changed her mind.

'I'm in trouble, here. I'm in a bad way. I know I am. Eileen's good, you know, but it's not fair. I've got to get something. Knock me out.'

'The trouble with most of the heavier sedatives is tolerance. You're on the maximum dose of temazepam…zomig…I don't want to…'

Like she was going to say something. Jump in, jump in, Bill. In case she changes her mind.

'What?'

'There's a new drug on the market. It's been licensed in America for years, but it's only just become available here...'

'I don't care. Can I have it?'

She smiled. He smiled.

Therapists don't bargain. Patients do that. They bargain with themselves, with their therapists, with their demons.

Thank God Bill didn't need to haggle, because if she'd held back, he would've cried all over again.

'Pick them up from the pharmacy,' she said. 'I'll put it through now. Seriously, though, I want to see you in a week.'

He felt bad when he left, dead on the hour. He'd left a Krama in there, and it had been worming its way between her thighs. But he didn't say anything. She didn't mind, and if he'd told her she might not have given him the pills, and he didn't want that, because he knew he was nuts, because the Krama had turned its mutant head to look at him and winked as it disappeared up her dress.

Some things you could tell your therapist. Others, you just had to shut up.

Thirty minutes or so later, with his prescription filled at the community hospital pharmacy, he pushed through the double doors. He turned and looked behind him. Red brick, same thing as always in relief above the door.

1897.

Told himself to stop doing it. Wasn't even good at maths, but he liked it. It was a good number, and not a time, which he liked more. It was a number the sun could never set on.

Like it had got to 18:59 and just kept rolling right along.

'Billy?'

'Hi, Eileen.'

'How'd it go,' she said, smiling, because he was smiling.

'Well, we'll see. Tonight. If you get a good night's sleep, it's because the sandman's hit me over the head with a great big hammer.'

'That's good,' she said. 'Let's hope so. If not, I'll try hitting you over the head instead.'

He laughed. Felt good to laugh, and for a moment, relaxed and hopeful because he had new pills, the laugh felt good.

'Come on,' he said. 'Treat you to a fry up on the way back. If that's OK…'

'Don't need to,' she said.

'I know. I want to,' he said, and got into the car beside her.

*

VII.

Bill took his evening cocktail and paced.

His cottage was small, not really the kind of place you could get a good pace on. He went back and forth between the kitchen and his living room, his feet slapping against the linoleum, then just the sound of the old floor boards creaking in the living room. They were the only two rooms downstairs.

He didn't want to pace upstairs.

He was hopeful, though, waiting for the pills to kick in. It was a hell of a cocktail. If this didn't work, he'd cry. He'd surely cry. Seemed like he cried a lot lately, but then most people, they saw the things he saw, the things that stopped him from sweetly sleeping and feeling better in the morning…well, most people, they saw those things, they'd be nuts, too. He wasn't the only one. He knew that. He knew other people thought they were bugged, the Government was out to get them, SHIELD and the Avengers, the fucking FBI, aliens, the dead risen, you name it, people had delusions about it. You couldn't put limits on insanity because imagination itself is limitless, and the intellect is able to create a more vivid canvass than all the stars in the sky.

Bill knew he was nuts, just as he knew if he could slow down those chemical reactions firing in his brain, slow those thoughts that were like nebula being born each second in his brain, he'd be just fine. Just fine.

He'd be fine in the morning, he thought, and hit his head on the wall because he'd just drifted off while he was pacing.

'Yes! Yes,' he cried and laughed and shook his head. His nose was actually bleeding.

He wiped it on his shirt then pulled his shirt over his head without undoing most of the buttons. He held the shirt to his nose but it was just a trickle.

He put the shirt straight into the washing machine and sat at the table, thinking of having a cigarette, but then thinking about falling asleep halfway through and burning his house down. Might be a way to go, but he might take Eileen with him…and he wasn't ever going down that road. Not now, not ever. Not fucking ever. E-fucking-nuff, he told himself and jumped, because he'd just fallen asleep at the table.

He laughed, a little laugh that caused more blood to trickle from his nose, but it didn't matter because he was stumbling as he walked up the stairs and fell into bed, in a dark bedroom, didn't even put the lights on. Just hit the top sheet, top off in a cold bedroom with frosted windows, trousers and shoes still on from his day out, and fell into a deep beautiful sleep.

*

VIII.

Bill woke to the sound of screaming coming from the wall.

He imagined he heard *them*, screaming at him to let them back in, like the new drug had blocked off the hole in the wall.

But it wasn't them. It wasn't him, either.

His head was so groggy, for a second, he couldn't figure it out, whether it was a dream, or the wall, or his head. But it wasn't any of those things.

It was Eileen.

It sounded like someone was killing her.

Still he couldn't do a fucking thing about it, because his legs wouldn't work. He tried to shout out, but couldn't.

Bill, fucking…come…fucking…on.

He loved the old lady, and someone was killing her. In as much as he could think, someone must have broken in. She was being hurt.

'Billy!'

Sheer terror and she thought to call for him.

'Caa…'

He pushed at the sheets with all his strength. The scream was losing power.

How long had she been screaming?

Was she dying?

'Come…' He pushed, grunting, straining but not getting anywhere.

'Come on!' Got to his feet and pushed himself up from the floor when his legs gave way, turned to the landing and the man standing there in the dark, who hit him in the mouth with a fist like a sledgehammer and he was out again, out 'til the morning, and into a nightmare so real he wasn't afraid of the things in the wall anymore. Not them, but the man.

*

Part Two

Something there is that doesn't love a wall...

Robert Frost
From *'Mending Wall'*

IX.

It was dark, still, but there was light in the sky...morning coming. For a second Bill was happy, happy with a full night's sleep and no terrors. No Yik, No Krama. No Hatheth, crawling into his brain.

But then, both his arms were numb and his foot hurt. He wasn't sure which was more irritating, but through the haze of his evening cocktail of drugs he couldn't work up much enthusiasm to worry about it.

They're not numb, Bill, his mind dredged up after a few minutes.

You can't move them because someone's tied your arms up. That pain in your wrists? Your biceps? That's rope.

It's not dark, either, because you can sense light, but the light's behind this sack over your head. You're on the bed, your arms are tied...

Someone hit you in the mouth last night. Knocked you out cold.

'Eileen!'

He could speak, alright, he could scream. His mouth hurt but the pills took the edge of it, off all his pains.

Shit. His pills. His pills...what time was it?

Eileen...Eileen...sorry...can you hear my thoughts? Can you hear me, through the wall? I'm going to come...if I can...

Of course she can't hear you. The wall's in the way. The man who hit you in the mouth?

Bill.

He's still here.

'William,' said a voice. Thick and full of gravel, like…a car, driving up a path, something heavy. A van.

'Don't try to fight it. The rope will get tighter.'

It was confusing. Was the man talking through the wall? To Eileen…or to him?

He tried to think while the man spoke, telling him to stay calm because the pain would get worse if he struggled. The man must be talking to him, but he couldn't figure it out. Couldn't think through the haze.

He tried to think through what was going on, how badly Eileen was hurt…how badly this man hurt her…how he was missing his pills and if he did how soon 'til the low beasts came…?

Then his mind kicked in.

Eileen was screaming when this man was in his house.

There were two of them.

Fuck.

He struggled. The man pulled the hood off and punched him in the nose and he was out again.

*

X.

Bill woke. Light was failing and night was coming on.

His face hurt. His foot hurt. He didn't remember…then he did. Didn't know why his foot hurt when he'd been punched in the face, but he'd probably hit it on the way down. But his foot and his face – they were small problems. He had a bigger problem, and he was standing in the shadows, the thick shadows of the darkness rising.

'Now,' said the man, standing in the shadows behind the misty light coming through his frosted windows. 'Here's how this is going to be. We're going to have a talk. Long or short, up to you. But we're going to have a talk and we're not going to have a struggle. Are we?'

Bill nodded, pain shooting through his broken nose. 'My pills…'

'Later,' said the man. 'I'm talking, so fucking shut up,' he said, and the gravel in his voice could hurt.

Bill bit down, trying not to cry.

'If you play up, I'm going to teach you. Remember being a teacher? Well, it's like that. Except, you know, with pain. Maybe I'll kill you, maybe I won't. Depends on you. You understand?'

'No,' said Bill.

The man laughed, a growling, frightening thing.

'Good,' he said.

Bill heard the man dialling. Like on a mobile. A couple of beeps only, as though the number was on speed dial, not like he'd had to put it in from scratch.

'Cut her finger off,' he said. 'Just one for now.'

Beep, connection cut, and Eileen screamed through the wall. Bill jumped.

Was this…was this real?

The scream went on and on. Bill had never heard a scream like that, but he imagined someone, a man, the other side of the wall. He could imagine more than he wanted to...secateurs, a knife, scissors...

He struggled and pushed and swore but he was tied down tight. The scream carried right on, and he couldn't do a thing about it.

'You bastard! You fucking sick cunt! Fuck! Let me…fuck! Fuck!'

'Good. Listening?'

'Fuck off!'

'Shut up, William. Shut up now, because there are some rules to this, and you need to listen, in case you make a mistake. Hurt yourself, you know? You're important to us, but don't…'

'Fuck off!'

The man was across the room in an instant and Bill got the sense he wasn't tall, but built, really wide, strong. The man slapped him so hard he saw spots for a second, right up on the ceiling, floating. He tasted blood.

'Don't interrupt. I was saying, don't make the mistake of thinking you're so important to us that we can't do without you. Now, are you listening?'

Bill nodded.

'Good. Good boy. Eileen, right?'

Bill stared at the broad shape back in the shadows.

'Answer me. Let's start out right, OK? Make this easier?'

Like he was a reasonable man, but as sick as Bill was, he wasn't stupid.

He nodded again.

'Here's the deal. You do something that I'm happy about, I won't hurt you, OK?'

Bill remained silent.

'You do something I'm unhappy about, I hurt you. Sometimes, when I feel like it, I'm going to hurt Eileen. Get it?'

'You fucking bastard…'

'Swearing, see? I don't mind that. That's kind of understandable.'

The man stepped forward, immensely broad, but short, and leaned in, putting his blunt face forward. Bill tried to pull back, but couldn't go far enough. He was bound tight down against the bed and could only twist his head. Totally captive. Totally helpless.

The man grinned, and Bill saw that he was chewing, behind that grin.

He poked out his tongue, and resting on the end of it was a little mangled something. Something Bill couldn't understand.

Thought of the pain in his foot, and then, right after, that the morsel on the man's tongue could be a toe, a small one, like a little toe. Like his little toe.

He screamed and the man laughed, that sick grinding thing that made Bill puke. He didn't know if it was his toe or the realisation that it was his toe the man was eating, or the laugh.

Could have been all three, but it didn't matter, because night was falling, and he hadn't had his pills.

The man laughed and carried on laughing, then he stopped for a second and Bill heard the sound of a man swallowing a tasty morsel.

Night comes quickly in the wide open spaces of the country. Night, and the low beasts. But he didn't have to worry about them now, because this man, this low man...he was eating him...

Bill wondered how much he'd already eaten and puked again, then, the last of the light failed and it was just Bill and the man in the dark.

*

XI.

It wasn't a crawlies or a creepies night. Bill hadn't had his meds. He didn't have Eileen to chase his nightmares away. Him and Eileen were living the nightmare, right now, and it didn't need crawlies and creepies to make it so.

He could see the Hatheth skittering, chitinous, segmented legs clacking and clattering as they swarmed from the hole in the wall. In among them the slow slimy forms of the Krama slithered across the floor, drawn by his blood, aiming for his toes…his missing toes. They'd lap at him, worm their way into his blood.

He didn't realise but he was screaming and crying and railing against them, trying to pull his foot back, but they were coming, they were coming and they'd eat him from the feet up, until they were sated, and the Yik could come, and God, God, God help him, Marlin? No God. No.

'No. No…God…fuck…Jesus…'

'Poor William. Poor, poor William.'

Screaming from next door, Eileen, shouting something…like 'it'll be alright, Billy'…trying to help him even though she was being tortured, just like he was.

It pulled him up sharp. If she could do that…he could deal with it. He could…

But the man stopped him, leaning in his face. He gulped, swallowed another of Bill's toes.

Picked up one of the Hatheth in his big thick hand and stroked it. It preened. Like it was home. But this wasn't *the* man. This wasn't him.

'What?' he said. Patients bargain, he thought. Don't talk to him. But he needed to know. How could it be? How could he see…unless…unless…

The Hatheth really were real…not just a sign on sickness, like the doctor told him, like he believed, sometimes, in a roundabout way during the day…they were really real. Really here. The wide man could see them. They fucking *liked* him.

'What? How?'

'You think you're the only one, William? The only one that sees them?'

The wide man shook his head.

'Back,' he said, and the creatures swarmed backward, crawling and sliding up the wall, back where they came from.

'Be a good boy, William. Maybe I'll won't let them at you.'

'Please,' said Bill. Realised he was crying again. Sobbing. Not from terror, this time, but with gratitude. This man could keep them back. He loved him.

This man ate your toes, some part deep inside Bill dredged back up. So long ago you forgot already? Don't be fucking stupid, Bill. Don't trust him. Not for a second. He's not the man, but he's something. He's something, alright. Don't fuck with him.

'I'll do anything,' said Bill, despite the voice that existed deep down, where the circle couldn't catch him.

'Good,' said the wide man with a big grin. 'Good boy.'

He picked up the phone. Watched Bill's eyes in the dark, like he could see perfectly even though there was only the light of a weak moon.

'What? No! I've been a good boy! I'm a good boy!'

The man grinned again and hit speed dial. Bill screamed at him, thrashed. He wet himself, he struggled so hard.

The man spoke into the phone. 'Make her a cup of tea,' he said, all jovial, like he'd just been mucking about with Bill. Even in the dark Bill could sense the big man wink at him.

The fight went straight out of Bill and he even smiled back.

'Then cut off her ear,' he said.

'No! No! You sick fuck...you...' but Bill was sobbing so hard then that he couldn't speak.

He could only think, and wish. He wished he was whole, and unbroken. Then maybe he could deal with this. But he wasn't. He was a cripple, handicapped, and it had nothing to do with his maimed foot. His mind was broken and he couldn't deal with it. Couldn't take any more.

'Just kill me,' he said, and meant it. He'd meant it for a long time, and only then, listening to Eileen's screams and his own deep sobbing, did he know how long he'd wanted this, wanted to die, because he was broken and he could never be fixed, and sometimes you just have to put a broken man to sleep.

Then, 'How deep does it go, Billy boy?' said the man in from the shadows, but Bill didn't understand.

The world was upside down and Bill didn't understand anything right then but pain and terror.

*

XII.

Bill's schizophrenia first presented when he was sitting his final exams in university. Back then, he'd been a confident man. Maybe he'd had a little charisma. He hadn't gone into a mental hospital aged twenty-eight a virgin.

Maybe it was the pressure, maybe some drugs, but the drugs weren't a habitual thing, more the kind of fucking about experimental period that's just commonplace for students and younger people, going to festivals, hunting around among the cow turds for magic mushrooms on cold autumn mornings. That kind of thing, but he never put it down to the few joints he'd smoked or the couple of mushrooms he'd taken.

Psychosocial factors, not just genetics, not just drugs. That's what he'd learned since, back in the early days of his diagnosis. Two years had passed since that one and only admission (committal, if he was honest). In that time the fascination with diagnosis gave way to a kind of dog-tired, couldn't give a shit phase. It was hard enough, living with it.

He remembered the first time he'd had a freak out, and it hadn't had anything to do with a bad trip, though the feel of it wasn't far off. Like acid, being stuck in the circle, stuck on that magic fucking roundabout and unable to get off. Sometimes the schizophrenia crippled him so bad it was like being tied down, being tortured, waiting, wishing to die.

He'd been watching Newsnight when it had happened the first time. When he'd seen the other side of the wall.

*

XIII.

Newsnight wasn't really freak out material, but the talking head on the show really started talking. His head was massive to begin with. The presenter's jaw was overly large. His nose was prominent, broad, and shot through with broken angry blood vessels. All his features stood out bold and somehow it was frightening to look at. And then it came out of the TV. Hard, maybe, for people who don't have mental illness, or a history of drugs. Hard to understand the feel of a massive freak out.

The presenter's head grinned at Bill, then laughed. Bill scuttled back onto the sofa. He'd been sitting cross-legged on the dirty old carpet that passed for flooring in the rented house he shared.

It was just a head, but the thing was, it wasn't attached to the presenter's body anymore, but kind of floated, like Bill imagined 3-D should look like. But it wasn't 3-D. It wasn't some technical trickery.

The head was really there, looming larger and larger, coming for Bill. Then it was there and the man didn't try to eat Bill. It wasn't anything terrible. But he kissed Bill on the cheek and spoke.

'They're coming, Bill. They want you. They need you. That's the news, Billy boy. That's the news on the hour.'

Bill squeezed his eyes tight shut but the head didn't go away, it just took on an orange hue like a cold room lit by a coal fire. The light distorted through his eyelids, but eyes shut or open, the man wanted to be seen.

And through it all, things crawled over the presenter's face. Later, Bill knew their name. It just came to him, what those horrible creatures were called.

They were the Yik, and they were many.

Bill's flatmate, David, he remembered, or Richard, came back from the pub and found him screaming and holding himself like a frightened child in the corner of the living room, his arms around his knees, hiding behind the sofa.

Bill tried to explain it to his flat mates, the day after. The cold light of day, and studying for a degree in history, a bunch of 'friends' from the course he shared a flat with…it hadn't been easy. None of them really did drugs. None of them knew what a bad trip was.

Fuck, most of them had only ever been drunk.

He may as well have been trying to explain the cosmos to an ant. Maybe he had been because you just couldn't explain something so large to something so small, he figured, but he figured wrong, because he hit the nail on the head, and the head was pretty damn big.

Looking back at it later, he'd hit the nail on the head, but missed the whole body of the nail, sunk down into the wood like it was. But by then he was long gone, and Bill Hunter that was broke.

'It's like a bad trip,' he told his flatmates. 'Like being stuck on a roundabout. You can't get off. It's a crazy fucking carnival where the horses on the merry-go-round are nailed right through with poles and your feet slip in the blood. The music isn't music, but horses screaming. Well, the newsreader's head came out of the television, and it was covered with bugs, like, millipedes, and, I remember thinking, Yik, Yik. Kind of while that was going on, things came out of his mouth and he was talking to me, calling my name…and right? I'm not that important. How would the newsreader know my name? But he did, and it's me that he wanted…'

Bill went on like that for a while longer, but it was only the day after and he was still on kind of a come down from a massive burst of chemicals fucking up his brain.

His flatmates called the doctor. The doctor gave Bill some pills to calm him down during his exams. It worked for a while.

That was the first time he saw the Yik, and he was right there with them. The Yik came from the walls and covered the wide man in his bedroom in the now, the present, the *real*.

The low beasts crawled and caressed his skin with their myriad limbs, like they were making love to him, that wide man, that *low* man.

Bill didn't know how long he'd been out, but it was light out again and the Yik were there right now.

In the daytime.

*

XIV.

'Please. God, please. Please. Let me take my pills.'
'What,' said the man, 'You can't handle it?' He plucked one of the Yik from his forehead and popped it into his mouth, crunching it up between his blunt back teeth, just like he'd crushed the marrow from Bill's toes.

'You're not the only one he wants. There are others, you know that right? You think you're that important?'

Bill was terrified. Didn't want to ask. Because he knew, but he had to ask.

'Who?'

'You know. Don't make me angry again. I swear. You don't want to,' he said, shaking his head.

His hair was receding, but otherwise Bill couldn't tell the man's age. He was just…massive. It was the one and only defining characteristic.

Bill nodded. Didn't need to go any further, nor wanted to.

'What do you want?'

'I thought you'd never ask,' said the man with a grin. There were pieces of the Yik stuck in his teeth. 'Been wasting my time, eating your toes, while Silo over there has been fucking up your girlfriend. You could've just asked straight off.'

'You could've just told me,' said Bill, but even in the midst of fear he knew there was no point in arguing with a psychopath.

There were different levels, even for nuts. Schizo's were top tier, but then psychopaths…a whole other playing field.

Bill had no doubt the man would kill him in an instant, if he wanted to. Like he'd said *eating your toes*. Hadn't said *eating a toe*. Bill didn't look down, because he couldn't handle it. Eating your toes.

Like maybe he'd eaten all of them.

Bill couldn't handle one more thing. Couldn't take the man standing there, his face crawling with Yik in the daytime. Couldn't handle the thought of Eileen next door, with the one called Silo. Not knowing what was happening to her.

'I'll do whatever you want. Don't hurt me anymore. Please. Leave Eileen alone. She doesn't see them. She doesn't know…please…'

'This isn't all about you, Bill. Never was. Not where the man's concerned. He's got long plans, see? He sees fucking long.'

'Please, just let Eileen go.'

'She's already gone. Went in the night. Couldn't take it.' And the man was smiling. Smiling and showing all those fat teeth, it seemed like, and Bill was angry. Good and fucking angry.

But he was tied down and although he knew, just knew, that the man didn't carry a knife or a gun or anything like that, he was also sure that this man didn't need weapons.

But if Eileen was dead already? He couldn't…couldn't believe it.

'If I…' he started, but then he wondered.

Did it matter if he lived or died?

He couldn't follow through on the thought, because right then the man punched him on the side of his head. Hard enough to ring his bell, but not put him out again. He shook his head while he groaned, the room swimming.

Was he losing blood, too? He thought maybe he was. But he wouldn't look down. No way. He couldn't see what had happened to his toes. But then he was going to have to be brave, wasn't he? Because Eileen was gone.

Because he was thinking hard all the time, and right at the top of those thoughts racing around his brain was one simple phrase, like the circle in his head, but this time it felt good and he didn't want to break it.

I don't want to die, the mantra ran.

A scream came from next door, and he jumped, because he wasn't expecting it. The wide man laughed.

'Just fucking with you! Ha. Your face! Fucking picture. She's fine.'

He cocked his head, listening to the scream.

'Maybe not fine, but you know…still kicking.'

Bill thought maybe he was dead, or asleep, or having some kind of freak out, so he looked down.

It wasn't a freak out. All the toes bar the big one on his right foot had been bitten down to horrible stumps.

It wasn't a dream.

God help me, he thought, crying again, hating himself for crying. He knew he was going to die, and the Yik and all the rest of those things, they didn't matter anymore. He knew they never did. It was all about the man.

The man. The man, always about him. It wasn't that Bill was important. He couldn't fool himself into that. But Marlin wanted him and he was stuck in his land now, the land of the other side, the other side of the wall, where he lived.

*

XV.

It wasn't a dream. No dream was ever like this. Not even during his most acute episode had things ever been this bad.

Could they get any worse?
Was there any chance it could get better?
He couldn't fool himself. The crazy man was eating him. All the things he was afraid of the bugs doing to him, and they were just crawling around. It was this man that was the threat. Wasn't anything to do with the circle. He wasn't having an episode. This hadn't anything to do with stress.

The man's phone rang. He picked up and moved back into the shadows in the corner and listened. Grunted.

He hung up and loomed over Bill.

'I have to go out for a minute,' he said, and for some stupid reason Bill's heart leapt, because it was a chance, a half chance. But then hope could be a sneaky bastard.

'You …well…doesn't matter what you do, really. Do what you like. You aren't going anywhere. Scream all you want. Nobody's coming. Just me, coming back. Believe that?'

Bill nodded, careful not to let his hope show in his eyes. Defeat. Despair. That was all he wanted the man to see.

A Yik fell from the man's face and landed on Bill's chest. He barely flinched.

'Well, be a good boy, then,' said the man and turned to go.

Before he reached the stairs, he turned back.

'Just one thing,' he said. 'One thing to think about while I'm gone.'

Bill felt terror then, because he imagined the wide man stepping across the room and eating more of him.

But he just asked a question, and that was somehow worse.

'How deep, Bill? Think on that.'

'What? I don't...' understand, he wanted to say, but the wide man was gone. No big fanfare, just heavy footfalls, receding down the narrow old stairs, and the front door slamming.

Bill waited.

He waited longer, wondering how long he'd have to wait to be sure. Wondering if he'd wait too long, and the man would come back, and he'd miss his chance.

Wondering if the man had really gone, or if this was just another sick game.

But the mantra, I don't want to die. I want to live. I want to live.

It ran through his head. He couldn't die. Not here.

And not because Eileen was still alive, but because he wanted life. He never knew how much until right then, bound, his toes eaten, his face bloodied.

He wanted to live, so he strained and wriggled and heaved as hard as he could. He cried because it hurt. He wanted to shout, to give himself one last push, one almighty effort, like a muscleman pushing a bar laden with weights toward the sky. The cry of a man who wouldn't give up.

He bit down instead, so hard a tooth cracked, and then something gave in his shoulder with a horrible crunch, like he'd just managed to break his own bones.

Thing was, he had, but now he could get his arms out of the bonds.

He laughed, but slapped his hand over his mouth, because the man had only gone next door.

Eileen.

Suddenly he understood the urgency. He could run, hide, maybe. Fight, get a knife, hit the guy with it, maybe get lucky. But it wasn't about him, not anymore.

He was broken, because he pushed himself to his feet and didn't scream when he landed on his mangled foot, didn't scream when he crushed a Hatheth under his heel.

Something was different, if only while he did what he needed to do. And for a moment, he felt the hand of God, his Eye, looking down on him, and God help him if that Eye didn't burn, didn't look like a lake of fire.

His shoulder burned, his nose and the whole of his face, and his foot...Jesus, he thought, looking down at his foot. He didn't know how he was walking, but more than that, how he was walking across a carpet of the Hatheth, crunching them underfoot, and not screaming. The hand and the Eye of God. He had made his gaze and his loving caress, like Eileen always said he would.

It felt like he was in the heart of the storm, and that was precisely what insanity was, and sometimes, it was just the right place to be.

His foot hit the first riser, his bad foot, and he did scream and tumbled, crashing, down the stairs.

*

XVI.

Bill Hunter had never hurt himself badly in his thirty years of life. He didn't know how seriously he'd injured his shoulder. He couldn't tell if it was broken, but when he hit the wall at the foot of the stairs he thought it was for sure.

He cracked his toes and blood started to pour out on the carpet. Thank God it was carpet, or he'd slip and break his arse, too.

He turned and looked over his shoulder, but the low beasts hadn't followed him down the stairs. He could have cried again, but this time he was angry, just plain angry, and somehow the anger was keeping the fear at bay.

Fear of them, and fear of the wide man's return.

He didn't know how long he had. He dragged himself up, his right arm pretty much useless, and stumbled into the kitchen.

He pulled out the drawer, tipping the whole thing to the floor in his haste. Then he collapsed onto his knees and rummaged through, until he found the biggest knife he could.

It was a bastard getting back up again, but he did it, just like he managed to steel himself to walk out into the cold light of day and across the fence to Eileen's and kill the men that had tortured them, or die trying. He pushed onto the door, though, and it wouldn't budge. In his anger he didn't try twice, think maybe the man had locked him in, but smashed the knife into the glass above the bottom panel.

The knife bounced back and didn't even make a mark. When he looked more closely, he saw what he took for a fine winter day wasn't anything of the sort. It didn't move as he did. Someone had painted his windows with an exact replica of his views.

He stared for a moment, dumb, unmoving. Forgetting Eileen and low beasts and torturers, with a cold chill deeper than anything he'd ever known settling in.

He checked the other windows. All the windows.

Then he dropped the knife and sat at the table with his head in his hands, because then he knew he really was fucking nuts.

Unmoving, unchanging, scenes on all the glass. Just paint, and not even onto glass, because they weren't windows at all, but brick.

His whole house was surrounded by walls.

*

XVII.

In the year up until the end of his first life, before he broke, Bill's condition steadily worsened. He never did end up in a room with white leather pads on the walls, but he did end up with a court order sectioning him and a nice enough single room in a bungalow with a key pad on the door.

It was in the year building up to his short residential stay that he first saw the man.

The man, the Marlin, came to him through the walls.

The Marlin lived in *all* the walls, and no matter where Bill went, whether it was the school room, or the bathroom, or the staff room, there were always, always, walls.

It was that year that the man started to run Bill's life, and the same year that Bill refused to follow orders anymore.

And God, that was hard, because you don't refuse the man and get off easy, and the man was the only one that mattered. The low beasts had a king, and Marlin was his name.

*

XVIII.

To start with, Marlin mainly got angry when Bill spoke about him. Then, later, he was angry when Bill even thought about him. But toward the end, toward Bill's breaking, he was very angry, because that was when Bill began to write about him.

Bill wrote on his walls at home. He wrote about Marlin in the margins in his students' homework.

Bill found out just how angry the man could be during one break time in class when the wall shattered. Brick flew across the room, crashed through the big second floor window. A shard of brick opened a gash across Bill's forehead.

He ducked down and covered himself with his arms as brick fell through the red brick dust cloud.

Marlin stepped through the wall.

'You tell them,' he said, in some kind of voice that was feral and erudite and made the two things one, 'And I'll have them eat you all. Every inch of you…you, your students, all the teachers. I'll fucking teach you, Bill. I'll teach you,' he said, leaning that horrible long face of his right into Bill, so far in that Bill could feel his warm stinking breath on his eyeballs. 'I'll teach you the meaning of fucking discretion,' he said.

Bill had no choice but to sit still, biting down hard, while the Hatheth and the Yik and the Krama crawled over him, and when break time was over and Marlin was gone, trying not to scream while the low beasts slithered and slid and clattered and clamoured among his students, everyone of them ignorant of the horrors in their midst.

'Reading, today,' he said. 'Chapters 3 through 8,' he said, and that was all he said for the whole lesson, because he had to bite down and bite down hard.

Somehow, he made it through fifty minutes without screaming.

At the end Marlin came back in.

The Marlin nodded.

Said nothing, then both the man and the low beasts were gone.

*

XIX.

Bill didn't write about Marlin for a month. Didn't think about *them*. Whenever Marlin came he put him in a circle, like a fairy ring, he imagined it, to stop the wicked elves breaking through.

He bought an iron horseshoe and wore that on a leather strap beneath his shirt for a while, but it was heavy and rubbed the seven he'd etched into his chest, so he didn't wear it all the time.

When a drug addict goes back to his smack, he hits it hard. An alcoholic doesn't fall off the wagon on a single shot of malt, but on a bottle of cheap shit whiskey from the corner shop.

Insane people don't do things by halves, either. If you don't break all the way, you're not insane.

Bill was on the way to breaking, perhaps snapping, after that hard month, when he began writing in the margins, again, writing on the walls in his apartment, trying to keep Marlin away, stop him breaking through.

'Marlin can't get through here. Seven.'

After everything he wrote seven. He gave all his students 7 out of 10, because seven protected him.

But really, it didn't work. Never does.

That was when he snapped all the way. The cracks in the wall came earlier, back when he'd been a student and the head first came out of the television, but the real cracks appeared when he began on seven and he shattered when he was caught breaking into the school and stealing his students' papers.

*

XX.

Bill smashed the window to the staff room with his fist, in which he held an iron horseshoe.

On his chest a seven carved with a compass, to hide himself from Marlin.

He cleared the window sill of glass and boosted himself up and over. The keys to the locked cabinets were in his front left pocket, because Marlin was right handed and if he snuck up behind him he wouldn't be able to get them.

But he didn't want to use the key, in case Marlin heard him. Marlin could break through walls, come out of doors. The power of Earth was making him stronger. But seven could hide you from him and iron could keep him back.

Bill crawled across the glass, keeping low so Marlin wouldn't see him, trying to be quiet.

'Shh,' he told himself. 'Silent, silent, seven and seven and seven and seven...'

Over and over, he spoke the magic number while the glass cut his palms and his knees.

He couldn't get a good swing hidden on the floor, so he stood, eyes closed so he could listen.

'Careful sevens,' he said, and punched at the locked cabinet with his horseshoe clutched in his fist like a forked jaw against the evil eye, his talisman and his ward both.

The lock broke and the files tumbled to the floor.

There was a file in cabinet in which he knew he'd written about Marlin. He didn't remember what he'd written, and Marlin didn't know, but he needed to get it, and get it fast, because the Hatheth were in his mind. Marlin would know, soon, maybe, 7 and IRON couldn't stop the Hatheth, couldn't stop the elf king, the Marlin man with his long sight and his long plans and his long, elegant body like a sword.

He mashed the horseshoe at the papers, like an eraser, mashing and tearing the papers until there was nothing left but shreds.

The alarm was pounding in his ears, but he didn't hear it. He heard the footsteps though, and Marlin was behind him.

'Smash it, William. Smash it. I'll have them eat you. I swear it.'

Bill turned and roared at him. Marlin's head nearly touched the ceiling, but iron would burn him, hurt him.

He lashed out with the iron, hitting out, again and again, but Marlin just backed away, and then he caught Bill's arm. He was unbelievably thin, but strong enough to wrench Bill's arm behind his back.

Marlin was sneaky, though, and tricked Bill into thinking the policeman wrestling with him wasn't a policeman, and when he snarled and swung it was the policeman who fought him, not Marlin. He took the horseshoe away, and then another policeman came and between the two of them they restrained Bill while he screamed and raved and ranted and bled from his chest through his shirt as the scabs over seven broke.

Bill spent two months in hospital after that, and Bill that was died. A new Bill was born. One with anger caged, ruled by fear. A man sitting with just one toe on his right foot and a broken shoulder in a room surrounded by walls.

But he still had the scar of 7 on his chest and an older 7 on his arm, and he laughed a little while the answer came to him, there at his kitchen table. Of course the answer was seven.

*

XXI.

Darkness was a way off. Still around five o'clock. Bedtime was seven. Winter or Summer, didn't matter. His father put him to bed at seven and seven was the good time. It was the bad time, too, because seven was when he got up. Winter or Summer.

Five o'clock, now, and winter, and it was dark outside while Bill sat at the kitchen table.

Even though the vista was just a painting on brick, darkness still fell and real or not Bill could feel it coming.

He carved a seven on his right arm, his left hand working fine. He carved a seven on his left, right over the old scar tissue, though his right shoulder was broken and making his hand work was hard.

The good seven and the bad, working together, because it was dark now and he was thinking about Marlin, and Marlin wouldn't be happy.

He didn't think the wide man was coming back. He was just a Hatheth a Krama a YIK a fucking Yik.

But time for thinking about the low beasts was over. He needed to break down the walls quickly now, through to Eileen's, because she was screaming again.

*

XXII.

All of Bill's garden tools were outside. He had a sledgehammer out there. He might be able to break through the wall with that, but then his right arm didn't work and he couldn't get to the sledgehammer anyway.

He couldn't see a way through the wall, but then there was a hole in the wall already, wasn't there?

He just needed to push, to squeeze, but it wasn't any different to breaking his bonds on the bed and pulling himself to his feet. He needed to make himself smaller.

He walked up the stairs on unsteady feet. His right foot pained him and his shoulder swung loose in the socket. With the hand that held the knife he steadied himself on the wall while he climbed.

The broken bonds still lay on the bed. He ignored them, because he was free of those. They didn't matter anymore, but the man was still pulling the strings.

Maybe it was him, next door, working on Eileen.

He took a deep breath, trying to calm himself while the old familiar terror of the night rose.

He closed his eyes for a few seconds, then opened them again and looked at the wall.

He looked at the hole, where they'd bitten through the plank he'd nailed down. Stared long and hard and thought about how to do it. Thought himself small.

Knelt before the hole and pushed his head at it. Pushed a little harder.

Something cracked and it felt to him like he'd just crushed the Hatheth that rode his mind. Then his head was in the wall. Just his head. His shoulders were stuck.

He remembered reading about a cat, and how if a cat could get its head through a hole its body could follow. He didn't know if it was true. Didn't know if it worked for men and women but then he had to try, didn't he?

It was full dark in the wall and he couldn't see anything at all. Suddenly he knew time was tight, because he could hear the scrabbling in the walls, and they were coming, coming for him.

Maybe the low beasts weren't the root of the problem, but they could still break through to the other side.

He had to be quick, before *they* told Marlin where he was.

It was pitch black in the wall and of course the low beasts were real. He could almost feel the Yik sucking at his maimed foot, lapping up his blood and sucking his marrow.

A cry came from his lips, but in the dark it was swallowed whole.

The Hatheth were only in his mind, but Marlin wasn't. Marlin was real, and Marlin could do things to him that the Hatheth and Krama and Yik could not. Marlin could push him into the wall. Keep him there, in the other realm, the realm on the other side of walls, where the circle made of daisies, the fairy ring, couldn't hold him.

The hole squeezed down on Bill's neck, but he pushed, his feet behind him ruffing the carpet in his bedroom, his foot crying out, his shoulder grating…but then his shoulders were through and he was in the wall, because once his shoulders pushed through the hole crumbled to nothing and he was out, into Eileen's beautiful house.

*

XXIII.

Bill stepped into Eileen's house and touched her things, like he was keeping a grip on reality. It wasn't an obsessive thing, but a comfort to touch something so solid, things with a history and weight and solidity.

His mind hurt, and he knew that even though he'd left his demons with Dr. Richards he hadn't had any medication for some time. Perhaps for days. He had no idea how long had passed, how many nightfalls had been and gone. He knew he'd be in trouble if he didn't get his meds, and soon.

So he touched things as he walked. Eileen's bed, her wardrobe, her walls. The wall he'd stepped through, crawled and pushed and pulled through, was solid again. Good solid brick. No holes in it. No holes at all.

He'd never been in Eileen's bedroom. Why would he have ever stepped in here? There was a valance over the bed, floral, and a painting of a flower on the wall behind him. The wardrobe was good solid wood. Maybe Georgian, Edwardian, something like that. The cottages had been built in 1906, and though Bill didn't really know when Edwardian or Georgian was, he figured the wardrobe could well be as old as the house. Maybe even came with the first owner.

A book was open on the bedside cabinet, pages down, so she knew which page to start at when she picked the book up again.

All natural. All as it should be.

He touched the nightstand, wardrobe, chest of drawers. Touched the walls, safe, here, touched the bed. Touched everything in the room.

But no blood. Not a drop.

And, something jarring, something he didn't understand.

There were speakers set into the corners of the ceiling. Like a surround sound system.

Cold, now, chilly, with no shirt, he stepped onto the stairs, carefully, taking as much weight as he could on his left leg.

*

XXIV.

Downstairs, cold, but not thinking of the cold, hungry, but not thinking of food.
Bill hit the bottom floor and walked over cold tiles, somehow soothing on his maimed foot.
Unconsciously he fingered the seven on his right arm, not thinking about how his foot hurt, or his shoulder grated every time he took a step and his arm swung loose in the socket.

On the kitchen table was a laptop. An Apple, or Mac, or whatever they were called. It was plugged into a speaker.

There was no screen saver. Just a moving box on the screen.

He leaned closer. The box said 'click me', but when he tried to catch it with the mouse it moved away, so he never got any closer to clicking it.

He hit return instead, and found it was a screensaver, after all, but a stupid joke one.

There was a program open on the laptop. It had sound files on it. He clicked the first and Eileen's scream filled the whole house, making him jump.

Now goosebumps rode his back and his spine tingled. Fear, now. Fear, like when the low beasts came for him, because Marlin was fucking with him now. Marlin was angry, because he'd been through the wall, because there was no hole in the wall this side.

But there were walls. He had to get out. Into the fields, where there were no walls.

Had to get out.

But what if Eileen's house was walled in, too?

Where was the wide man?

'Fuck,' he said, and looked down. He'd put the knife he'd brought with him on the kitchen table. He picked it up again, angry at himself for going unarmed, even if only for a minute.

He hurried to Eileen's front door and tried the handle.

'Thank you,' he said to no one in particular, because the door opened.

*

XXV.

He stepped through into another nightmare. Tears came running down his face because nothing was real and he was insane. Insane and broken and flat out fucked.

He found himself not in Eileen's front garden, with her hanging baskets, with the road out the front, or the fields, or anything like that.

He was in the community hospital. Dr. Richards sat in front of him, her legs crossed.

Her knees were level and her calves ran parallel to each other. She had on a red dress with white flowers, and a bow on her breast.

Bill realised he could think breast, now. Because he wasn't on his pills. Because he was straight and his mind was firing, firing on all cylinders like a fucking race car, and he could feel the fat of his own breasts, and his gut hanging over his trousers, but he could feel he was in a room with a beautiful woman, too.

'Would you like to sit down, William?' she said.

'Yes,' he said, smiling. 'Nice to see you. You look…beautiful,' he said, feeling slightly foolish, but meaning it, nonetheless.

'Thank you. What a nice thing to say. You can smoke if you want. If it would make you feel more comfortable.'

'I didn't bring my cigarettes,' he said.

'You can have one of mine,' she said, and passed her his packets. They were menthol, but he didn't mind. He was just happy to smoke. She leaned forward and lit his cigarette for him. He looked down her dress, at her cleavage. She caught him looking, but she smiled, and everything was alright.

Part Three

We live on a placid island of ignorance in the midst of black seas of infinity; and it was not meant that we should voyage far.

H.P. Lovecraft
The Call of Cthulhu

XXVI.

'Do you ever get angry?' she said, as she lit her own cigarette.

Bill thought about it and smoked for a while. There was nowhere to tap his ash.

'Eileen was being tortured, and I think…yes…I'm angry. I was angry, then, but I don't think it was real. But then…'

He waved his mutilated foot at her. 'If it's not real, what the fuck happened to my toes? I need something, Doctor, because I can't see what's really real and what's pearly peels.'

'Are you aware you're talking in rhyme at this time?' she asked.

'Are you aware there's a Krama licking your cunt?'

'Hunting my cunt?'

'No, licking. They lick.'

'You're being rude, William. You're never rude. Not you. Never rude…nor crude.'

'No, no, I'm not…' he said.

She switched her smile back on and stood, leaning over the chair, looking at him over her shoulder. She hitched up her skirt and showed him where the Krama was wriggling. But it wasn't erotic. It was horrible and sickening.

She was smiling still, though, so he played along, because he didn't want her to stop smiling. Not in this nightmare that never ended.

For he was sure it was still the same nightmare, and if the Krama were here, the other low beasts were, too, and they were *his* minions. His *legion*. His *goblins*, he thought, gobble-gobble, as he looked right in the Krama's eye, giggled, then stopped. What if she really could read his mind?

'We had this conversation before, and your mind is dredging it up. You remembered we talked about seven?'

'No,' he said. 'I don't remember…I remember you asking if I got angry…'

He looked down at the knife clutched in his good fist. Shrugged. Apologetic.

'Seven makes you angry, Bill. And yet…you have it carved into both arms…'

'Seven's the good number,' he said, shaking his head.

'And the bad, too. Remember? Remember?'

And the thing of it was, he did. Seven to bed, Seven to rise, and an insane father, raising him like father like son but in that dark old house, so dark he couldn't run, and the shadows grew long and roundabout his feet while all the while the Krama swirled and swarmed around his meat, licking and biting, the Yik inviting...

So inviting.

He remembered the fear. And yes. The anger. The anger when he'd finally been left alone, at his father, for going away, and at himself, too. Yes, he was angry at himself, and that was because he'd driven his father away. That was when he started cutting, but it was with the seven on his chest that he'd gone into hospital for the first time.

*

XXVII.

At first the police brought him to a cell, after he'd tried to erase the evidence he'd written about Marlin on the school papers. But they looked into it, and didn't have to look far. They found his writing on the walls in his rented apartment, took statements from his colleagues and his two remaining friends.

Bill sat on an uncomfortable bench, the only furniture in the cell.

He'd noted the pink door on the way through. He noted a coffee machine, and he had such a thirst on him but wanted to go to the toilet at the same time. He was terrified, not of the policemen, who were rough but really real. Solid and firm so he wasn't afraid that they could break down the walls in his cell.

The Marlin could, though.

He wished he had a pen, or some chalk, or even a burnt match to write with. To stop him.

But he couldn't because the Marlin, the man, was already in there with him.

He sat next to Bill on the bench.

'You've been a bad boy, William. Bad. I had plans for you. I told you, didn't I? I was your friend.'

'We can still be friends,' said Bill, and hated himself for the pleading in his voice, that sick child, wanting, needing love.

Marlin shook that long head of his, perched atop his impossibly thin neck.

'No, William. No longer. No more.'

'Don't…don't…please…'

He begged, because he knew. The Krama slurped and licked and covered with slime. The Yik, hideous, like millipedes, they crawled up his nose and his arse and into his cock, sometimes.

But the Hatheth, they burrowed. Under his skin and into his brain.

Marlin called them and they came. They scuttled up his arms and his legs and burrowed into him, through his clothes.

Bill screamed and scratched until he bled.

That was how the police found him. Screaming and covered in scratches and blood.

The assessment didn't last long, when the psychiatrist finally came. Shortly after, the hospital.

*

XXVIII.

'Goodbye, Dr. Richards,' said Bill, as she got on her knees and pulled her dress down, showing him her breasts. The Hatheth were in her and pushed against the skin of her breasts from the inside. Her skin rippled and he felt sick rather than excited.

He pushed her away from him, because he was free of them for a time…his nightmares had jumped to her, and for a while he could think. He could remember. Remember the old hospital, where his new life began and the old Bill Hunter, the Bill Hunter that was, died and was reborn like a crippled phoenix from the ashes.

The corridor was wide and long in the community hospital. The entrance and exit both was at the end. He knew he could not pass through the entrance and exit to the outside from the clinic. Dr. Richards barred his way, holding him back like she'd always done, with pills and with fucking talk therapy.

Dr. Richard's grasped out at him, clutching desperately and managing to dig her nails through his trousers right into his left nut. He pushed her again, hard enough that when she fell she yanked him and a few seconds later that sickly feeling in the pit of his stomach started, like he'd been kicked between the legs really hard.

He couldn't do anything about the pain. The pain was constant. His foot, his cuts, his scratches and breaks.

He put one mangled foot in front of the other and set out along the wide path to freedom. Toward the other side of madness.

*

XXIX.

Bill scratched at the Hatheth crawling under his skin and tried the number pad again. He was sure it would be some permutation of 7. He tried 1906, 2608, both of which added to 16, and 1 and 6 made seven. He tried this for three hours, and the staff in the mental hospital allowed him to do it, because there was no way he could ever get out. The combination was impossible to guess and it didn't matter how long he tried at it if it kept him docile.

A big fat bear of a man watched him try, then eventually grunted and walked away.

A woman came up to him.

'Have you got a cigarette, please?' her voice almost begged, but he was engrossed in his task.

She went away, and he only stopped when dinner came out, because he was ravenous all the time.

A man slapped him in the face when he was eating, and he hit him back with the edge of the tray, cutting the man's forehead.

He was a broad man and could easily have broke Bill in two, could have crushed him between his arms if he wanted to.

But the broad man just cried. While he cried Bill took the man's food and ate that, too.

The meal was shepherd's pie, or cottage pie. Bill couldn't taste the difference in the meat, but it tasted just fine with a little salt and pepper. Everything tasted fine with salt and pepper. He tried salt and pepper on the trifle that came for pudding, but he didn't like it.

He still ate it, though.

The broad man bled and none of the staff had noticed. He tried to take Bill's trifle and Bill hit him again, even though he didn't like the trifle.

Mark, one of the nurses, held Bill down, and Lynn, another, injected him with something that made him sleep, and he slept for a long time. Every night they gave him different pills. For the first month or so he watched television in the common room until early in the morning, but then his mind couldn't take it anymore and he slept and ate and put some weight on that he'd lost during his breakdown.

He realised he was getting fat, and took to walking the length of the hall. He walked the long walk along linoleum floors, some kind of heavy duty thing. He wore his own clothes and his own shoes. In that first month he caught a veruca in the shower and he walked with a slight limp because it was uncomfortable.

Everyday Bill walked that long walk, past the crazies and nurses alike. People said hello to him and he said hello back. Sometimes people ignored him, or didn't even realise he was there, and he didn't say hello to them.

He thought maybe people could read his mind, and tried to be polite to everyone. He didn't hit anyone else with a tray.

Bill tried the number on the key pad every day. It became an obsession. Trying permutations of seven in some kind of simplistic numerological battle with an inanimate keypad that didn't give a shit how desperate Bill was to escape, escape from the Marlin.

But the thing was, the Marlin didn't come. He didn't see the Yik or the Hatheth or the Krama. He saw doctors and took pills and watched soap operas on the television in the common room.

He became friendly, after a fashion, with a young nurse named David. Or Richard. As he walked the halls in the community hospital and thought back to the mental hospital he couldn't remember the young nurses name. But it didn't matter.

The young nurse's face had been deformed. He had a great tumour, or growth, on his face. But he had good eyes. Like something beautiful on an elephant, a grotesquery with a sweet heart.

The nurse and Bill spoke often in those early days. Bill wouldn't speak of Marlin, because he wasn't there and he couldn't break into the hospital and it was refuge for him.

They spoke long and Bill thought all the while of the code to the door to freedom.

'Seven,' he told the nurse. 'That's the answer. People don't realise, but it's not three. Three's not the magic number. It's not pi. It's seven. Check the bible. Check it. I read it. I read Revelations. I read it. I read it.'

7, like the scars on his arms, like the scars on his wrists. The scars that kept the Marlin away.

Bill didn't realise how fucking nuts he sounded until he'd been in hospital for five weeks and things began to slow a little. He wanted to apologise to David, or Richard, whatever his name was, because he'd been nuts, but by then the nurse with the beautiful and ugly face had moved on.

*

XXX.

In the community hospital, half remembering, half dazed, Bill passed physiotherapy, passed reception, passed maternity, the fitness suite.

Finally, he reached a door. But of course, it was walled in.

He couldn't get out. Not this time. There was no hole in the wall to crawl through.

But there was a key pad. And the combination was the same as it always was, as he'd always known. He just had to be brave enough to use it, to get through to the other side, to escape this madness, this hospital, the other hospital. To escape seven he had to embrace it.

Was he ready?

No.

Was he angry? Yes. He was fucking furious. Marlin had so much to pay for, so much to pay back. He'd taken Bill's life. Bill had to take his. Had to stop it.

He tapped in the keycode with the tip of his knife.

1897.

Hit enter, and the door, the wall, buzzed. He pulled the door open and stepped through to the other side, the pathway to the end, maybe, or just another riddle.

He wouldn't know until he took that step.

*

XXXI.

When Bill stepped through to the other side, he knew he was insane, completely and utterly, because the land on the other side of Earth, on the realm that slid by, parallel, behind, in front…around…it couldn't exist. It couldn't be real. It could be nothing more than imagination, maybe an imagination that had travelled too far and over an uncharted border in the fabric of the world.

The sky above burned with fire, roiling like a blaze in a house catching the paint on a ceiling, rolling where fluffy clouds should be. The sky, the whole of it, as far as the eye could see, was red with flame.

This world needed no sun. But with no sun there were no trees and there was no grass. Without a sun this land could not sustain life.

It was why the Marlin needed the energy from the other side, from the Earth, because this was a land of imagination, a land of pure thought, and thought was its only sustenance.

Without thought it was just blasted endless wastes, an apocalypse in the making.

Bill travelled through the end of days, alone and barefoot and topless, and only then did he wonder what had happened to his shoes.

Surely he had worn them when he had fallen asleep, days, maybe months, maybe minutes ago.

But he wasn't wearing them now, and the burning landscape scalded his feet as he walked the endless miles across the wasteland. The fires cauterised the stumps of his toes, and he found that there was no pain, though he walked on with a heavy limp. He still held the knife in his left hand, and his right shoulder hung down low. He thought now that maybe it was both dislocated and broken, but self-diagnosis was a fool's game. You needed a trained professional for that. Someone to tell you what you couldn't figure out for yourself, because you can't see inside, you can't see the broken parts.

His feet covered yards, miles, leagues and fathoms, up, down, through, all the while walking with his ungainly rolling gait, like the flames rolling through the sky.

This world was hot, and he was glad he wasn't wearing his shirt. The shirt would have been soaked through, like his trousers and his underwear.

He realised that there was thunder, and rain fell, burning rain. His skin sizzled and blackened, and still there was no pain.

But he thought maybe this lack of pain was dangerous, just the same.

He began to run, with loping strides, made awkward by his lack of toes. He ran until he could breathe no more, while his skin and his hair caught fire and he charred. He felt the heat in his muscles and his arms curled up, his fingers became like claws as his muscles burned within him.

But there was a lake, a lake of fire, and God help him if it didn't look like sanctuary from the rain, like an oasis in a sun scorched desert, because he dived in head first and found wonder on the other side. A cessation of the fire, and cool beautiful, beautiful…peace.

*

XXXII.

Beneath the fire, a lake, beneath the lake, a palace, a palace that was dry and safe. A palace that looked a lot like a house he'd once known, semi-detached, him on one side, a woman named…Eileen?
 Eileen. Yes.
 And there she was, a queen in this cursed land of fire and thought.
 She was the woman on the throne, next to Marlin.
 The old woman who loved God and neighbour alike, loving Marlin.
 Obscenely, she was writhing and bucking, astride the long man's lap while the legion of low beasts cavorted and licked and sucked and entered, yes, that, too.
 'Hello,' grunted Marlin, and set Eileen aside. She moaned, she groaned, but he slapped her hard and she fell silent.
 'Hello, William. Welcome. Welcome to the world on the other side, the world across the bridge. The world behind the wall.'

*

XXXIII.

Marlin held out his arms, wide, like the sea waiting to pull a ship down into its cold embrace.

There were seven thorns on his crown, for he was surely the king, the king of his domain.

'Are you angry, Bill?' he said.

Bill shook his head, biting his lip. The low beasts were gone. Eileen was still panting, panting from her orgasm. Sweat beaded her brow and she smiled, a red welt on her face from her lover's slap.

'Just playing, son, just playing,' said Marlin, stroking Eileen's hair. She growled at him but he kept on stroking her hair, just like she was the family dog. A dog named Eileen, but nobody called a dog Eileen.

'Why did you do it?' said Bill. 'Why did you leave? Set the low beasts on me? I did as you asked. I didn't talk about you. I didn't!'

'I didn't leave, William. You pushed me away, remember?'

'No! No! I don't remember!'

'Aw, Billy, don't shout,' said Eileen. 'Be a good boy.'

And Bill was a good boy. He was…how old was he? He tried to remember, but when he dug back he couldn't. Couldn't bring it out. But he looked down and saw his hand, slender, barely covered in fine hairs, the skin tight and the muscles undeveloped. Long thin arms, like a pianist, but without the talent. The arms and hands of an adolescent.

'You pushed, William. Do you ever get angry, William? Are you angry now?'

'I hardly ever get angry,' he said.

He just needed some pills and all this would go away. But sometimes you have to go through the wall, even when there's no hole.

*

XXXIV.

'Come on, William. Come here. It'll be alright.'
Bill held the knife before him and approached.
'Oh, Billy. Bad boy,' said Eileen, seeing the knife for the first time. 'Billy, put that down right now.'
'It's alright, mummy,' said Marlin. 'The boy's got to learn.'
'I'm not angry,' said Bill.
'You're holding it wrong. Not like that,' said Marlin.
'You're nuts!' shouted Bill. 'You always were! You made my life fucking hell!'
Marlin laughed and took the knife from Bill in one swift gesture. Bill thought he couldn't be afraid anymore, but he could, faced with Marlin holding his kitchen knife.
Bill ran then, ran through the house, away from his crazy daddy, down to the kitchen. He tried the kitchen door which led out into the garden and safety, but it was after seven, it was bedtime and the door was locked. Of course it was.
The Marlin caught Bill round his wrist, his young hairless wrist, and swung him around to face him. The Marlin was still naked, naked from fucking Eileen, fucking his mother.
'Like this,' said Marlin, stabbing down into Bill's arm.
Then he pulled the knife out and flipped it for Bill to hold. 'You try,' he said.
Bill didn't move. Couldn't move. He was too afraid.

'Go on, son,' said Eileen, moping her thighs with a handkerchief.

'Come on, son. You try,' said Marlin. But Bill's hand shook so badly and he was so terrified and yes, hurt, that he couldn't take the knife from his father. So his father showed him again.

'Like this, Bill!' he said and stabbed down again.

Bill looked down and the wound, one atop the other, the second cut deeper and longer, looked to him just like a 7.

'Take it!' cried his father. His father was actually crying now, and real tears rolled down his face, but those tears were hot when they dropped onto Bill's arm, hot like burning rain falling down and scolding his skin.

If he felt another of those tears on his skin he would char, he would burn.

Bill's hand shook as he held it out, dripping blood onto the tiled floor of the palace.

Marlin placed the knife in the boy's hand. 'You try,' he said. 'Come on. You can do it.'

'No,' said Bill, William, Billy. 'No,' said the boy, but his father grabbed the hand holding the knife and forced it down, laughing all the time as Bill stabbed and stabbed and stabbed, laughing because the man, the Marlin, always was insane.

*

XXXV.

'Do you ever get angry, William?' asked Dr Richards.
  'Hardly ever,' he said.
  'It's OK to be angry,' she said.
  'I'm not…'
  'Angry with your father.'
  'I'm not,' he said. But he was. Just as he was angry with himself. And always would be.
  Because he stabbed and stabbed and stabbed.

XXXVI.

The digital clock on the night stand read 7:37 PM when Billy pushed the door open.

His mummy leapt to one side and Billy saw that there was a Yik between his mother's legs before she closed them, and a Krama between his father's legs, rearing up, the thing's slimy head pointing at him.

'It's alright, son,' said mummy. 'Daddy and me, we're just…playing.'

His daddy was laughing.

His daddy was always laughing. There was something broke inside daddy. Once, when Billy was younger – too young – his mummy had called it 'Shitsofrenia'. Billy had never looked it up, but then he was only eight years old then and more interested in playing football than reading in the library. He figured it was some adult word to explain why it smelled so badly after daddy had been to the toilet.

But the thing, the Krama, reared up at him and he was afraid, so he ran, ran to get something to hit it with. His daddy ran after him, and the Krama chased him, and he thought about that Krama, hurting mummy's Yik, and yes, yes, God help him. He got angry.

Did he have the knife already in his hand? Had he run to get it, or did he already have it?

He couldn't remember now. Couldn't remember anything but the Yik and the Krama, and the Hatheth, crawling over his mother's breasts, the flesh roiling with them.

Couldn't remember anything but the knife and he took it up in his hand and it was made of steel but there was iron in there, too.

He took a knife from the kitchen drawer and turned as fast as he could. His father pulled the knife from him and stabbed down.

'Like that, William,' his father, his daddy, the man, said. 'You're holding it wrong,' he said and stabbed Billy in the arm again.

Then he flipped it and gave it back. Laughing.

'You try,' he said.

Afterward, Billy thought the scar on his arm looked a lot like a seven.

*

XXXVII.

'Do you ever get angry?' said Dr. Richards, but she knew what the answer was, and so did Bill.

'Yes,' he said. 'Yes. I do.'

'At yourself?'

'Of course. Self-harming. Self-hatred...a cry for help...I know all that. Just...'

How could he explain? He'd died that night, back when he was too young to know any better. Back the first time he'd found the Yik and the Krama and then forgot. Yes, he forgot.

How could he explain what it was like to be so dead inside, so black, so numb, that to cut and cut was to feel *something*. Sometimes, even when he'd been cutting, it hadn't hurt. It had felt like a release. His skin was so numb he couldn't feel the knife going in, carving 7 on his chest, on his arms and into his wrists. How could you explain death to the living and how good it could feel to bleed?

'I wanted to feel again,' he said with a shrug. He could try. He could talk right up until the hour was up, but what use would it be? Dr. Richard's couldn't see the Hatheth, their legs clicking like fingers and squeezing like a man's hands on a firm pair of breast, on his mother's fucking tits, their chitin armour unable to feel that sweet flesh.

How could you explain the Hatheth but for invading hands, invading the Yik, stroking the Krama? How could you explain the low beasts to this woman with her red dress with white flowers and her bow and her knowledge that she was sane and he was insane, but of course he wasn't. He never had been, because he'd seen the land on the other side of the wall and no one else ever could. He'd travelled over, seen the kingdom of the Marlin and he'd returned with his scars, yes, and he couldn't feel, yes, but he wasn't dead inside like the blind.

'Feel what?'

'Alive.'

'And your father? Are you angry with him?'

'Yes,' he said. 'Yes, I am.'

'Because he killed you?'

'What?'

'He ruined you, Bill. Don't you see that?'

'I killed him.'

'No, William. No, Billy. You didn't kill him. There are many different ways to commit suicide,' she said. She smiled, but he didn't understand.

'Suicide? I murdered him.'

Dr. Richards flipped her chart shut and uncrossed her knees. She leaned forward.

'There are many different ways of committing suicide,' she said. 'And just as many not to,' she added. She leaned forward and Bill saw her cleavage. She smiled.

'How deep does it go, Bill? How deep?' she said, smiling while those Hatheth writhed under her dress and under her skin. 'How deep, Billy?' she asked, but he couldn't answer because it was one hour and time was up.

'Goodbye, Billy,' she said.

He pushed himself to his feet and walked unsteadily in his uneasy gait, back to Eileen and the car and the cottage and everything else that waits on the other side. Back to the lake of burning fire and the kingdom beyond the wall, where the man, the Marlin reigns.

    End

About the Author

Craig Saunders is the author of over forty novels and novellas, including 'Masters of Blood and Bone', 'RAIN' and 'Deadlift'. He writes across many genres.

Craig lives in Norfolk, England, with his wife and children, likes nice people and good coffee. Find out more on Amazon, or visit:

www.craigrsaunders.blogspot.com
www.facebook.com/craigrsaundersauthor
@Grumblesprout

Also by Craig Saunders

Novels:
ALT-Reich
PIG (with Edward Lorn)
Ghost Voices
Highwayman
Hangman
The Dead Boy
Left to Darkness (The Oblivion Series #1)
Masters of Blood and Bone
Cold Fire
A Home by the Sea
RAIN
A Stranger's Grave
The Love of the Dead
Spiggot
Spiggot, Too
Vigil
BLOOD, DRUGS, TEA

Novellas:
A Scarecrow to Watch over Her (The Mulrones #1)
Death by a Mother's Hand (The Mulrones #2)
Flesh and Coin (The Mulrones #3)
Deadlift (The Mulrones #4)
The Lies of Angels
UNIT 731
Bloodeye
Insulation
The Walls of Madness
Days of Christmas

As Craig R. Saunders:

The Outlaw King (The Line of Kings Trilogy Book One)
The Thief King (The Line of Kings Trilogy Book Two)
The Queen of Thieves (The Line of Kings Trilogy Book Three)
Rythe Awakes (The Rythe Quadrilogy Book One)
The Tides of Rythe (The Rythe Quadrilogy Book Two)
Rythe Falls (The Rythe Quadrilogy Book Three)
Beneath Rythe (The Rythe Quadrilogy Book Four)

Short Fiction Collections:
The Cold Inside
Dead in the Trunk
Angels in Black and White
Dark Words

Printed in Dunstable, United Kingdom